SNOWBALL RUN

by Lisa Harkrader
illustrated by Lynne Avril

Kane Press
New York

Dedicated to Lee and Heather, my brother and sister, and all our childhood adventures—L.H.

For Ellie and Ben, my sledding buddies!—L.A.

Acknowledgements: Our thanks to Caitlin Coe, Science Educator, and to Susan Longo, Former Early Childhood and Elementary School Teacher, Mamaroneck, NY, for helping us make this book as accurate as possible. Special thanks to Meagan Branday Susi for providing the activities in the back of this book.

Library of Congress Cataloging-in-Publication Data
Names: Harkrader, Lisa, author. | Avril, Lynne, 1951- illustrator.
Title: Snowball Run / by Lisa Harkrader ; illustrated by Lynne Avril.
Description: New York : Kane Press, [2018] | Series: Science solves it! |
  Summary: Emmie learns about pulleys when she has to figure out a way to
  help her tired little brother climb up the sledding hill on a snow day.
  Includes science activities.
Identifiers: LCCN 2017046387 (print) | LCCN 2017015167 (ebook) | ISBN
  9781635920048 (ebook) | ISBN 9781635920031 (pbk. : alk. paper)
Subjects: | CYAC: Snow--Fiction. | Pulleys--Fiction. | Force and
  energy--Fiction.
Classification: LCC PZ7.H22615 (print) | LCC PZ7.H22615 Sn 2018 (ebook) | DDC
  [E]--dc23
LC record available at https://lccn.loc.gov/2017046387

10 9 8 7 6 5 4 3 2

First published in the United States of America in 2018 by Kane Press, Inc.
Printed in China

Science Solves It! is a registered trademark of Kane Press, Inc.

Book Design: Michelle Martinez

Visit us online at **www.kanepress.com**

 Like us on Facebook
facebook.com/kanepress

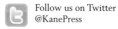 Follow us on Twitter
@KanePress

"Springdale School," I whispered. "Please say Springdale School."

"Is that it?" My little brother, Owen, pointed at the TV.

"Nope," I said.

He pointed again. "That one?"

My heart thunked. "Not yet."

Snow piled up outside. Inside, Owen and I kept our eyes fixed on the TV.

SNOW DAY
SCHOOLS CLOSED

Owen pointed. "What about that one?"

"Yes!" I gave him a fist bump.

Finally! The name we'd been waiting for. Springdale School.

"Snow day?" said Owen.

"Snow day," I said.

Thump, thump, thump.
Someone knocked on the door.
It was Booker, my best friend. Lucky for me, he lived next door. Luckier still, he had his sled.
"It's time for Snowball Run!" Booker said.
"I get to go, too," Owen told him. "I'm big now."

5

Mom bundled Owen in his snow pants and coat.
He looked like a marshmallow with legs.
"Stay with Emmie," Mom told Owen.
"If he gets tired," she told me, "bring him home."

Home? I'd been waiting a whole year for the snow. I'd been telling Owen all about going sledding on snow days. We were going to have the best day ever. We couldn't come home.

"He won't get tired," I said.

"We'll take care of the little guy," said Booker.

"I'm big now," said Owen.

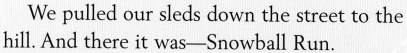

We pulled our sleds down the street to the hill. And there it was—Snowball Run.

Every kid in the neighborhood was out. They scrambled up to the flagpole at the top of the hill. They slid down, laughing and shouting.

Booker and I grabbed our sleds. We grabbed Owen's hands. We set off up the hill.

We plodded. We plowed.

Owen's short legs barely made it through the deep snow.

Finally! We reached the top.

Booker climbed on his sled. Owen and I climbed on ours.

"Ready?" said Booker.

"Ready!" said Owen.

We pushed off. Our sleds teetered on the edge for a second.

Then they tipped down the hill, and suddenly we were flying.

"*Woweee!*" Owen held tight to my legs.

We whooshed and swooshed. The wind
whipped our faces. Snow billowed up around us.
We skidded to the bottom and tumbled off.
"Do it again!" said Owen.

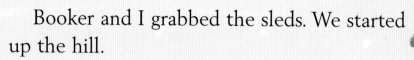

Booker and I grabbed the sleds. We started up the hill.

"Emmie!" Owen cried. "I'm stuck!"

I looked down. Owen had toppled over backward in the snow. He waggled his arms and legs like a turtle on its back.

I pulled Owen to his feet. He slumped
against me.

"Being big is hard," he said. "Can we go home?"

I blinked back tears. I promised Mom I'd bring Owen home if he got tired. But I wanted us to have the best day ever. And we'd only slid down once.

"I know!" said Booker. "We'll pull him up the hill."

"Yes!" I gave Booker a fist bump.

When you want to move something, you push it or pull it. A push or a pull is called a **force**.

We put Owen on the sled.
Booker and I pulled and pulled.
We plodded and plowed.
At last we made it to the top. Booker and I
stooped over, trying to catch our breath.
"Being big *is* hard," said Booker.

We climbed onto our sleds. We pushed off.
We flew down the hill and landed in a giggling
heap.

Then Booker and I turned around. We stared
up at the hill.

Booker groaned. "I can't pull Owen up to
the flagpole again."

Flagpole? I sat up. I watched the flag flapping at the top of the pole.

"I have an idea!" I said. "And I know who can help."

I hauled Owen out of the snow.

"Let's go home," I said. "We'll make cocoa. *Then* we'll make plans."

We found Mom in the kitchen. I told her my brilliant idea.

"Every morning at school, we raise the flag on the flagpole," I said. "We clip the flag to the rope at the bottom. Then we pull it to the top."

"It's on a pulley," said Mom. "The rope goes around a wheel at the top of the pole. When you pull one side of the rope down, the other side goes up."

I knew Mom could help us. She built houses, so she knew this stuff.

"We need a pulley for Owen," I said.

He nodded. "I need to go up."

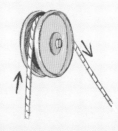

A basic pulley is made up of a wheel with a groove around it. The groove guides the rope or cable.

We took our cocoa out to the garage. Mom found a couple thick ropes and a big pulley.

"This should do the trick," she said. "It's not as big as the ones I use at work. But at work we have to lift steel beams. They're a lot heavier than Owen and his sled."

Booker eyed the ropes. He eyed the pulley.

"This will make it easier to pull Owen?" he said.

"This will make it a *lot* easier to pull Owen," said Mom.

Mom held up the pulley. "It lets you pull down, instead of up. When you're pulling down, you can use your own weight to pull. That's easier than dragging your weight up."

"Our weight *plus* Owen and the sled," said Booker.

Lifting heavy objects is hard! A **pulley** is a simple machine that can help you out. It can decrease the amount of force you use or it can change the direction of your force. Pulling down is easier than pushing up!

The more pulleys you have, the easier it is to lift an object!

←Easy

Easier! →

Mom grabbed the pulley. Booker grabbed the ropes. I grabbed Owen. We trekked back to Snowball Run.

The pulley had a big metal ring on top.
Mom looped one rope through the ring. She
tied it tight to the flagpole so the pulley
wouldn't move.

The other rope was long. Mom slid it
through the pulley. Booker and I each took an
end of the rope and went back to the bottom
of the hill.

We tied one end to the sled. Owen climbed on board. Booker and I grabbed the rope's other end together.

We started to pull.

The sled started to slide.

Booker and I pulled and pulled. Owen and the sled slid and slid. We pulled down. Owen slid up.

When he reached the top, Booker and I scrambled up the hill after him. We climbed on our sleds. We pushed off.

Gravity is the force that pulls people and things down to Earth. When you lift something up, you work against gravity. When you pull something down, you work with gravity. That makes pulling down easier!

"Woweee!" Owen's voice rang out over Snowball Run.

We skimmed over the snow. The wind whipped our faces. Owen laughed and squealed.

We skidded to a stop at the bottom, and Owen tumbled off.

"Do it again!" he said.

Soon, the neighbor kids gathered around our
rope pull.

"That's really smart," said one girl.

"Can we try it?" said someone else.

"Sure," said Owen. "I'll show you."

We got in line. We all took turns. Whoever
pulled a sled up got the next turn sliding down
Snowball Run.

We pulled up. We slid down. Then we
turned around and did it all over again.

"It's just about time for dinner," said Mom. We grabbed our sleds. I grabbed Owen's hand. We set out toward home.

As we walked, Owen leaned against me.
"Thanks, Emmie," he said. "That was the best
day ever. I love being big."

I can predict!

I can go up!

THINK LIKE A SCIENTIST

Emmie thinks like a scientist—and so can you! Scientists use what they know, from experience or research, to make predictions. Emmie observed the flagpole and was able to predict a solution to her sledding problem. Making a prediction is an important part of any science experiment!

Look Back

- Look at pages 18–19. What problem did Emmie and Booker need to solve? How did Emmie use what she knew to help them?
- Review the definition of a pulley on page 22. Explain how a pulley could make it easier to get Owen to the top of the hill.
- Re-read pages 25–26. Did the pulley work? How do you know?

Try This!

Think about ways you could use a pulley like Emmie's in your home or classroom to make your life easier. Draw a picture of how you would use the pulley in your home or classroom.